The Heaven of Animals

Nancy Tillman

FEIWEL AND FRIENDS

NEW YORK

With all of my heart, I believe it is true
that there is a heaven for animals, too.

Sometimes I think that they already know,
all of the animals . . . just where they'll go.

Haven't you noticed them drift off and stare,
lift their soft noses, and gaze into air?

I think that maybe it's heaven they see . . .

beyond what their wishes
could wish it to be.

When dogs get to heaven
they're welcomed by name,

and angels know every dog's
favorite game.

They race to the corners of heaven and back,

and everyone gets a turn leading the pack.

When kitties arrive on their soft kitty paws
they are even more lovely to look at because
when they bathe up in heaven, their fur is so fine—
they stretch out their toes and just let themselves shine.

They perch on a limb of their very own tree.
It is amazing how far they can see.

Then they play and they purr, and they yawn and they nap
in their own ray of light in their favorite lap.

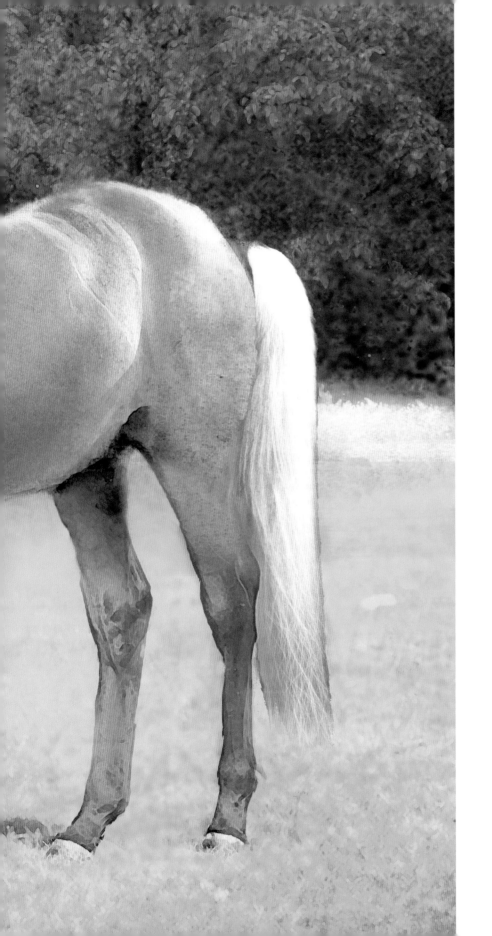

Horses in heaven are never alone,
and grass is much sweeter than
grass here at home.

Whenever they want to, horses
can snack; as soon as they nibble,
grass grows itself back.

Sometimes a horse just wants to have fun,
so he and his friends kick their hooves up and run.

When it is thundering high in the sky,
horses in heaven are galloping by.

Days often end
in fantastical hues—

marmalade oranges . . .

butterfly blues.

Sometimes at twilight,
in indigo skies,
animals gather
to play with fireflies.

Sometimes they dance
with the angels, or sing.

Heaven changes everything.

But the love that you have for your animal friends
is always the same—that love never ends.

It makes itself known in all kinds of ways.
It floats all around them, or settles and stays.
And when angels whisper in animal ears,
it is your voice that each animal hears.

You'll grow older; I will, too.
That's what people always do.

But when you meet your friends again,
they'll see you as they saw you then.

And you'll find they always knew
how much they were loved . . .

and how much they loved *you*.

To Dane, Merlyn, and Griselda. I'll see you on the other side.
—N.T.

A FEIWEL AND FRIENDS BOOK
An Imprint of Macmillan

Feiwel and Friends books may be purchased for business or promotional use. For information on bulk purchases,
please contact the Macmillan Corporate and Premium Sales Department at (800) 221-7945 x5442 or by e-mail at specialmarkets@macmillan.com.

Library of Congress Cataloging-in-Publication Data Available

ISBN: 978-0-312-55369-2

Book design by Nancy Tillman and Kathleen Breitenfeld

The artwork was created digitally using a variety of software painting programs on a Wacom tablet. Layers of illustrative elements are first individually created,
then merged to form a composite. At this point, texture and mixed media (primarily chalk, watercolor, and pencil) are applied to complete each illustration.

Feiwel and Friends logo designed by Filomena Tuosto

First Edition: 2014

10 9 8 7 6 5 4 3 2 1

mackids.com

You are loved.